NURSERY RHYMES

Rookie
**Nursery
Rhymes**™

Children's Press®
An Imprint of Scholastic Inc.

Library of Congress Cataloging-in-Publication Data

Names: Farias, Carolina, illustrator. | Lewis, Anthony, 1966- author.
Title: Sing-along nursery rhymes.
Description: New York, NY : Children's Press, an imprint of Scholastic Inc.,
[2016] | ?2017 | Series: Rookie nursery rhymes | Summary: Includes three
traditional nursery rhymes, illustrated by two different artists.
Identifiers: LCCN 2016005482| ISBN 9780531228760 (library binding) | ISBN
9780531229620 (pbk.)
Subjects: LCSH: Nursery rhymes. | Children's poetry. | CYAC: Nursery rhymes.
Classification: LCC PZ8.3 .S6144 2016 | DDC 398.8—dc23 LC record available at http://lccn.loc.gov/2016005482

Produced by Spooky Cheetah Press
Design by Book & Look

Printed in China 62

2 3 4 5 6 7 8 9 10 R 25 24 23 22 21 20 19 18 17 16

Illustrations by Carolina Farías (It's Raining, It's Pouring), Anthony Lewis (The Itsy-Bitsy Spider and Mary Had a Little Lamb), and pp 6–12, 14–20, 22–28 (wooden bar) Venimo/Shutterstock

TABLE OF CONTENTS

IT'S RAINING, IT'S POURING

Illustrated by Carolina Farías

Listen to the audio here:

http://www.scholastic.com/NR1

It's raining,

it's pouring,

the old man

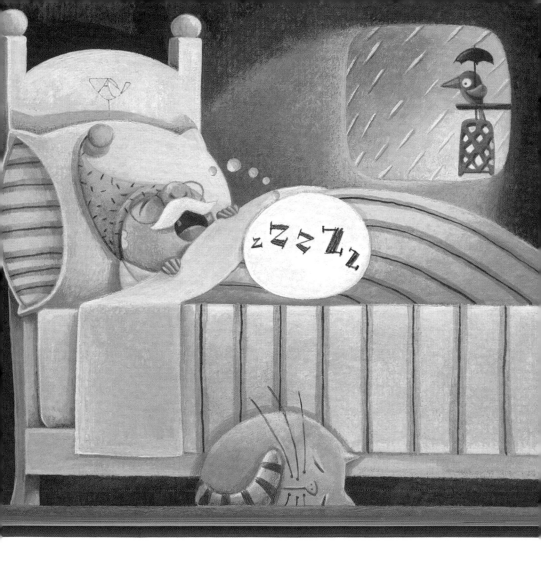

is snoring.

He bumped his head

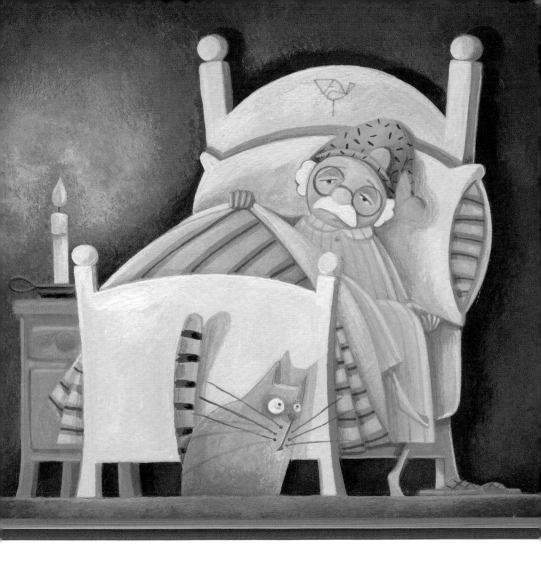

and went to bed

and couldn't get up
in the morning.

THE ITSY-BITSY SPIDER

Illustrated by Anthony Lewis

Listen to the audio here:

http://www.scholastic.com/NR2

The itsy-bitsy spider

climbed up the waterspout.

Down came the rain

and washed the spider out.

Out came the sun
and dried up all the rain.

Then the itsy-bitsy spider

went up the spout again.

MARY HAD A LITTLE LAMB

Illustrated by Anthony Lewis

Mary had a little lamb

with fleece as white as snow.

And everywhere
that Mary went,

the lamb was sure to go.

He followed her to school
one day,

which was against the rule.

It made the children laugh and play to see a lamb at school.

FUN WITH
NURSERY
RHYMES

FUN WITH It's Raining, It's Pouring

Pages 5 to 12

A lot of animals are pictured in this nursery rhyme, both outside in the rain and staying dry inside.

Look back through the book.

• How many animals can you count altogether? Can you name them all?

• How many times does the cat appear in the story?

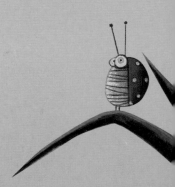

The Itsy-Bitsy Spider is pink, purple, and blue. She has two friends: a caterpillar and a ladybug. They are very colorful, too!

Go back and find them in the story.

- What color is the caterpillar?
- What color is the ladybug?

FUN WITH

Mary Had a Little Lamb
Pages 21 to 28

Mary's lamb follows her to lots of different places.

Look back at the pictures in the story.

- Can you name all the places Mary and her lamb go?

- Do you know the whole "Mary Had a Little Lamb" song?

Sing all the words!